ACCLAIM FOR COLLEEN COBLE

"Coble's atmospheric and suspenseful series launch should appeal to fans of Tracie Peterson and other authors of Christian romantic suspense."

—*Library Journal* review of
Tidewater Inn

"Romantically tense, but with just the right touch of danger, this cowboy love story is surprisingly clever—and pleasingly sweet."

—USAToday.com review of
Blue Moon Promise

"Colleen Coble will keep you glued to each page as she shows you the beauty of God's most primitive land and the dangers it hides."

—www.RomanceJunkies.com

"[An] outstanding, completely engaging tale that will have you on the edge of your seat . . . A must-have for all fans of romantic suspense!"

—TheRomanceReaders
Connection.com review of
Anathema

"Colleen Coble lays an intricate trail in *Without a Trace* and draws the reader on like a hound with a scent."

—*Romantic Times*, 4½ stars

"Coble's historical series just keeps getting better with each entry."

"Don't ever mistake [Coble's] for the fluffy romances with a little bit of suspense. She writes solid suspense, and she ties it all together beautifully with a wonderful message."

"This book has everything I enjoy: mystery, romance, and suspense. The characters are likable, understandable, and I can relate to them."

"[M]ystery, danger, and intrigue as well as romance, love, and subtle inspiration. *The Lightkeeper's Daughter* is a 'keeper.'"

"Colleen is a master storyteller."

A
HEART'S
*B*ETRAYAL

ALSO BY COLLEEN COBLE

SUNSET COVE NOVELS
The Inn at Ocean's Edge
(Available April 2015)

HOPE BEACH NOVELS
Tidewater Inn
Rosemary Cottage
Seagrass Pier

UNDER TEXAS STARS NOVELS
Blue Moon Promise
Safe in His Arms

THE MERCY FALLS SERIES
The Lightkeeper's Daughter
The Lightkeeper's Bride
The Lightkeeper's Ball

LONESTAR NOVELS
Lonestar Sanctuary
Lonestar Secrets
Lonestar Homecoming
Lonestar Angel
All is Calm: A Lonestar
Christmas Novella (e-book only)

THE ROCK HARBOR SERIES
Without a Trace
Beyond a Doubt
Into the Deep
Cry in the Night
Silent Night: A Rock Harbor
Christmas Novella (e-book only)

THE ALOHA REEF SERIES
Distant Echoes
Black Sands
Dangerous Depths
Midnight Sea
Holy Night: An Aloha Reef
Christmas Novella (e-book only)
Alaska Twilight
Fire Dancer
Abomination
Anathema
Butterfly Palace

NOVELLAS INCLUDED IN:
Smitten
Secretly Smitten
Smitten Book Club

OTHER NOVELLAS
Bluebonnet Bride

A
HEART'S
BETRAYAL

COLLEEN
COBLE

THOMAS NELSON
Since 1798

NASHVILLE   MEXICO CITY   RIO DE JANEIRO

Published in Nashville, Tennessee, by Thomas Nelson. Thomas Nelson is a registered trademark of HarperCollins Christian Publishing, Inc.

Thomas Nelson titles may be purchased in bulk for educational, business, fund-raising, or sales promotional use. For information, please e-mail SpecialMarkets@ThomasNelson.com.

Scripture quotations are from *The Holy Bible*, King James Version.

Publisher's Note: This novel is a work of fiction. Names, characters, places, and incidents are either products of the author's imagination or used fictitiously. All characters are fictional, and any similarity to people living or dead is purely coincidental.

Library of Congress Cataloging-in-Publication Data

Library of Congress Cataloging-in-Publication Data
Coble, Colleen.
Heart's betrayal / Colleen Coble.
pages ; cm. -- (A journey of the heart ; 4)
ISBN 978-0-529-10343-7 (softcover)
1. Widows--Fiction. 2. Pregnant women--Fiction. 3. Man-woman relationships--Fiction. I. Title.
PS3553.O2285H425 2015
813'.54--dc23
2014048238

Printed in the United States of America

15 16 17 18 19 RRD 6 5 4 3 2 1

For my brother Rick Rhoads,
who never let me lose faith in myself.

A LETTER FROM THE AUTHOR

Dear Reader,
    I can't tell you how excited I am to share this story with you! It's the first series I ever wrote, and it will always be special to me because writing was how I dealt with my brother Randy's death. You'll see a piece of my dear brother in Rand's character throughout this series. These four books were originally titled *Where Leads the Heart* and *Plains of Promise*. They haven't been available in print form for nearly ten years, so I'm thrilled to share them with you.

When my brother Randy was killed in a freak lightning accident, I went to Wyoming to see where he had lived. Standing on the parade ground at Fort Laramie, the idea for the first book dropped into my head. I went home excited to write it. It took a year to write, and I thought for sure there would be a bidding war on it! :) Not so much. It took six more years for a publisher to pick it up. But the wait was worth it!

This series seemed a good one to break up into a serialization model to introduce readers to my work. Even in my early stories, I had to have villains and danger lurking around the corner. :) I hope you enjoy this trip back in time with me.

E-mail me at colleen@colleencoble.com and let me know what you think!

Love,
Colleen

ONE

AUGUST 1866, WABASH, INDIANA

The ticking of the grandfather clock in the hallway echoed in the shrouded darkness of the parlor. Emmie Courtney sat on the black horsehair sofa, her hands clasped in the folds of her silk skirt. She stared into space as she desperately tried to imagine she was some other place, that the reason her friends and neighbors were gathered in her house on this sultry August day was something else entirely. The clatter of carriage wheels on the fine plank streets outside the open window couldn't drown out the beat of her heart pounding in her ears.

He can't be dead. I have to wake up. This is just a nightmare. A nightmare. She repeated the litany to herself as she closed her eyes to avoid the pitying eyes of her friends.

Only last week her life had been perfect. Married to a handsome, up-and-coming lawyer in the burgeoning town of Wabash, Indiana, her life seemed like a fairy tale come true. The War between the States was over, and parties and gay life were everywhere.

But now her dashing husband lay buried in a grave under the rain drizzling down outside. The nearly overpowering scent of the flowers massed around the room couldn't quite cover the stench of decay that had wafted up from the casket and permeated the room for the last few days. That undeniable smell told her quite clearly that this wasn't a nightmare.

Her neighbor Lally Saylors touched her shoulder. "Do try to eat a bit, Emmie, dear." She handed her a cup of tea and a small bowl of stew, then sat beside her.

Emmie took it and forced a sip of tea down her tight throat. "I still can't quite grasp it, you know. I keep expecting Monroe to come bursting in the door shouting for me to get my cloak and go for a drive or something. I don't think I'll ever forget the sound of the horses screaming as the carriage rolled over."

"You were lucky to get off with only a concussion."

"But Monroe—I needed more time with him." Emmie broke off, too choked to continue.

Her eyes misting with tears, Lally patted Emmie's hand. "I know, dear."

It had been three marvelous months. Emmie had lived securely in a love that she'd never before experienced, a love that shone from Monroe's laughing brown eyes whenever he looked at her.

"How did you meet? Sometimes it helps to talk about it."

Emmie smiled as the memory swept over her. "Things were always . . . difficult at home, and I often took off to walk along the river. My father had been particularly nasty one day, and I went to my favorite spot at Hanging Rock. I was sitting there wiping tears when Monroe stepped out of the shadows with a daffodil in his hand. He said no one as beautiful as me should look so sad, and he wanted to do something to make me smile."

"And did it?"

"No one could be sad around Monroe. He was always so full of life and laughter. He said his goal in life was to never see me cry again." Her throat thickened. "He would have been grieved to see me now."

"One only had to see how he looked at you to know he adored you." Lally took a sip of her tea. "Have you thought yet about what you will do?"

Emmie shook her head. "I haven't heard from Ben and Labe since they left for the Dakota Territory. I don't have any other family."

"I just hate it that you're here all alone, so far from your kin at a time like this."

Emmie nodded. She was used to it, though. She and her brothers had never been close, and after her mother died, her father was almost always drunk until his death three years ago. Emmie had grown up in a ramshackle country home just outside town, with the animals for friends. Her brother Labe had given her sporadic attention, but Ben ignored her except when he wanted something. Ben was obsessed with making the Croftner name stand for something other than "the town drunk." He would have approved of Monroe.

She'd never had a best friend and didn't really know how to have fun until Monroe swept into her life like a whirlwind. They'd married after a courtship of only six weeks, and after three months of marriage, she still felt she hadn't even begun to know her fascinating husband.

Now she never would.

She took another halfhearted nibble of her food. "I'll probably stay here at least for a while. The house is paid for, and we never seemed to want for money. Surely there is enough to live on for a while if I'm careful. Mr. Eddingfield is supposed to come out tomorrow to discuss my financial affairs." She cringed at the thought of facing Monroe's employer and his sympathy. All she wanted was to curl up here in the dark house and be left alone.

Somehow she got through the funeral and the burial until all the well-meaning friends and neighbors left the reception with promises to call again. She shut the front door, then lay down on the sofa. Through the open window she heard the shouts of children playing hopscotch across the street and the gentle hum of bees in the honeysuckle just under the window. The fecund scent of the Wabash River, just down the hill, wafted in with poignant memories of happy picnics with Monroe beside its placid waters.

How could life continue as if nothing had happened? She bit her lip as the hot tears coursed down her cheeks, then pulled the afghan down off the back of the sofa onto her shivering body. It was hot, but she couldn't stop shaking, a reaction to the trauma of seeing Monroe's casket lowered into that dark, forbidding hole in the ground.

She hadn't been able to sleep since the accident, but now she was so tired she couldn't keep her eyes open. The creaks and rattles of carriages outside on the busy street faded as she fell asleep, dreaming of Monroe.

The parlor was deep in shadow when she awoke. She gazed around in bewilderment, not sure what had awakened her. The clock still ticked in the hallway and carriages still rattled over the street outside. Then someone on the front porch banged the knocker again. Brushing at the wrinkles in her silk skirt, she lurched to the door. She felt disoriented and fuzzy-headed as she pulled the door open.

"Emmiline Courtney?" A young woman stood on the porch with a small boy of about two in her arms.

She was neatly dressed in a dark-blue serge dress with a demure white collar. Gentle brown eyes looked out from beneath a stylish though modest bonnet with a single drooping ostrich feather.

"Yes. May I help you?" The child reminded her of someone, but she was still too groggy from sleep and sorrow to place whom he looked like. And the woman's calm appraisal put her hackles up in some indefinable way.

The woman glanced away, then set her small chin and looked straight into Emmie's inquiring eyes. "May I come in? I have something of the utmost importance to discuss with you. It's about Monroe."

Emmie stared into the woman's determined eyes and nodded. "This way." She led the way into the parlor, then lit two more lamps and seated the young woman on the sofa before sinking into the matching armchair facing her guest. Discarded china from the funeral dinner still littered the smooth walnut tables.

Emmie rubbed her eyes. "I'm sorry for the mess. The funeral and all—" She broke off on a choked sob.

Her visitor nodded as she settled the little boy on her lap and removed her gloves.

"I'm sorry, I didn't catch your name." Emmie's gaze was caught by the pity in the woman's eyes. She caught a whiff of a faint lilac sachet as the woman pleated the folds of her dress nervously. She used to wear the scent herself, but Monroe didn't like it, so she'd switched to lily of the valley.

The young woman took a deep breath. "This is going to come as quite a shock to you, and I'm truly sorry for that. I'm Mrs. Monroe Courtney. Catherine Courtney. Monroe was my childhood sweetheart. We were married three years ago in Cleveland."

Mrs. Monroe Courtney. The words had no meaning to her. How odd that they were married to someone with the same name. Then the pity in the woman's gaze penetrated her stupor. Surely the woman didn't mean *she* was Monroe's wife? Beginning to tremble with an awful premonition, she stared at the woman.

At Emmie's silence, the woman tipped up her chin. "Surely you wondered why he never brought you to meet his family? He didn't dare reveal he was a bigamist."

Bigamy. There had to be some mistake. Emmie wetted her lips. "He said they were all dead. That they died in a train accident when he was seventeen." Emmie's lips barely moved as she spoke in a whisper.

Catherine's mouth tightened, and a flush stained her pale cheeks. "He has four brothers and three sisters. His mother and father are both in excellent health. They've been very hurt by his silence." She opened her reticule and drew out two pictures. "Here's a family portrait of Monroe with his father and the rest of the family. It was taken just before he disappeared. This one was taken after our marriage."

Emmie took the first picture and stared down into Monroe's familiar laughing eyes. An older man with a curling handlebar mustache sat in the middle of a group of young adults. There was a marked resemblance between Monroe and the other people in the photograph. They all had the strong jawline that made her husband so attractive, the same large, expressive eyes. The second showed Monroe with his arm around this woman, and she smiled up at him.

Something squeezed in her chest, and she handed back the photographs. "If you were married to him, why were you living apart?"

Catherine drew a deep breath and adjusted her little one on her lap a bit. "We had an argument. It was silly—over nothing, really. But he'd been acting restless and short-tempered for several weeks. He took off, and I never heard from him again. I saw his obituary in *The Plain Dealer* just this week. He didn't even know about Richard here." She indicated the little boy, who had his thumb corked in his mouth.

"Monroe was never very good at responsibility. Even as a child he enjoyed pretending to be someone he wasn't. There were spells when he'd take off, but he always returned in a few weeks. This was the longest he'd ever been gone. I heard he passed himself off as a lawyer here too. The truth is, he only got about halfway through law school before he grew bored and quit."

Emmie gripped her hands together. Monroe already married? Where did that leave her? She couldn't seem to take in the horror of her situation. *Bigamy.* The very word brought a wave of shame and nausea. Monroe had always seemed mysterious. That had been part of his magnetism. And it was true he was easily bored. But his eagerness for new adventures was part of his charm.

"You still have not shown me any proof of this marriage."

"I have an affidavit from his father and my marriage lines, of course. I will present them to Monroe's lawyer tomorrow. I can show them to you if you insist." She leaned down and pulled the documents from her purse. Keeping a hand on them, she showed them to Emmie.

Emmie read over the affidavit. There seemed little doubt the woman's claim was true. "What do you want from me?"

Catherine looked her over. "I wouldn't have come if it wasn't for my son. But my family is poor, and Monroe's father has been supporting Richard and me. But he's struggling too. I heard that Monroe had amassed a small holding here. It's only Richard's due that he inherits his father's possessions. You're young, and you don't have a baby to worry about. You can always go home to your family."

Emmie wanted to burst into tears and wail aloud, but she held her head up. There was pity in the woman's face. Emmie was sure Catherine thought she was a fool for believing Monroe's lies.

But who could have suspected Monroe capable of something so heinous?

Catherine shifted little Richard to her shoulder, then stood. "I'll leave you to consider all I've told you. If you need to contact me, I'll be at the Blue Goose Inn." She gazed down at Emmie's face. "I'm truly sorry."

Blood thundering in her ears, Emmie watched Catherine leave with a last pitying look. *That's whom the child looked like.* He was a younger version of Monroe right down to the pouting upper lip. She sat rigidly in the chair with her hands clenched. What was she going to do now?

TWO

As Emmie sat in the overstuffed chair in the law office of Taylor and Eddingfield, she felt as though she couldn't handle any more shocks. Catherine had left her documents with James Eddingfield, Monroe's employer, to check.

At his desk, Mr. Eddingfield looked through his wire-rimmed glasses and pursed his thin lips as he studied the documents. "These seem to all be in order. If I could discount her claims, I would. I sent a telegraph to Mr. Courtney yesterday, as well as to his banker for verification of her identity. I received an answer this morning. The woman is Monroe's real wife."

"Do I have any rights at all?" Emmie asked.

"I'm afraid not. Only what you brought into the so-called marriage. Your personal belongings and any dowry."

"I didn't have a dowry yet. The house Ben promised us as my dowry is still tied up until his debts are paid. I don't have any money until then." Ben had fled town after a scandal involving Sarah Montgomery and Rand Campbell. When the townspeople found out about his deceit, all his debts had been called in. Rather than face what he'd done, he had taken off out West.

James laid down the documents. "Unfortunately, the law is all on Mrs. Courtney's side. And she does have Monroe's child to consider." He rose from behind his gleaming desk and came around to stand in front of her. "I'm sorry, Miss Croftner."

Miss Croftner. With those words, the impact hit her and she shuddered.

Mr. Eddingfield reached down and took her hand. "Is there no one who would take you in? Your brothers, perhaps?"

She didn't like the feel of his moist hand or the way

he was looking at her, and she tried to discreetly pull her hand away. "No one. I don't even know where Ben and Labe are."

James squeezed her hand tighter, then lifted it to his lips. "I've always admired you, my dear Emmie. And, uh, tendered a certain regard for you. I would consider it an honor if you'd let me take care of you. There's a lovely little house on Sherman Street I own. Secluded and private. I could visit you there and see to all your needs."

The meaning of his words eluded Emmie for a few moments, but the greedy look in his eyes didn't. She gasped when she realized at last what he meant. She yanked her hand out of his grasp and rose shakily. "Mr. Eddingfield, please! I thought you were Monroe's friend—and mine!"

"What I offer is the best you can hope for once everyone knows you lived with Monroe without benefit of marriage."

Was there something about her looks that made men think she was a loose woman? She'd always wondered if she was truly a Croftner. Her raven-black hair and violet eyes were so very different from her brothers' fair hair and pale blue eyes.

Her face burned, and she wanted nothing more than to take a bath. "I did nothing wrong, Mr. Eddingfield. The fault does not lie with me."

His eyes narrowed to slits. "Perhaps. Who can say for sure what you really believed? At least that's what people will say. My heart goes out to you, my dear. I want only to help. I offer you a respite. If you can find it in your heart to receive my goodwill, I think we'll both be the happier for it."

She gathered up her belongings, bile rising in her throat, and stumbled toward the door. She had to get out of here. "Recently I've learned that the heart is a poor discerner of a prudent path. I must reject your offer, Mr. Eddingfield. Please, let's no longer speak of something so shameful."

"You'll come crawling back when you see no one in polite society will accept you," he shouted as she closed the door behind her.

A half hour later, drained and disheartened, she let herself inside the cool, dark house she'd called home for three months. Mrs. Hatters must have been here while she was gone—she could smell the faint scent of lemon and wax, and the house shone as it always did after her housekeeper's ministrations. It would probably be the last time Mrs. Hatters deigned to work for her once the town knew about her shame. Not that she could afford her now, of course.

Her steps echoed on the oak floor as she took off her bonnet and walked wearily to the parlor. The house seemed so empty and desolate. Was it just a week ago that it rang with voices and laughter at the elegant dinner party they'd had?

She looked around at her home. She'd brought so few personal belongings. According to Mr. Eddingfield, she wouldn't even be allowed to take enough to set up housekeeping elsewhere. Just her mother's cedar chest packed with a few linens, her own clothing, and a chipped Chippendale tea set that had belonged to her grandmother.

What was she to do? Where could she go? Could she find employment here in Wabash somewhere? But she had no skills, no special training. And what if Eddingfield was right and she was shunned by polite society, by the very people she'd thought were her friends? She buried her face in her hands and gave in to the tears she'd managed to keep at bay for the past two days. She'd tried to be strong, stronger than she felt. But fate seemed determined to keep her down in the mire. She was just the daughter of the town drunk, after all.

After a few minutes she raised her head and wiped her cheeks. There had to be an answer to her dilemma somewhere out there, but where? She bolted upright as a sudden thought took hold. What about Sarah Montgomery? She'd run into Sarah's mother-in-law, Margaret, at Beitman and Wolf's dry goods counter last week. Margaret had said Sarah was pining for some female companionship, and Margaret wished she knew of some young woman to send out to keep Sarah company.

Would Sarah welcome the sister of her ex-fiancé? She had always treated Emmie like an older sister and acted as though she genuinely cared about her. She'd even sent a congratulatory letter when she'd heard of her marriage to Monroe.

Emmie rose and went to fetch her bonnet. At least there was hope.

THREE

SEPTEMBER 1866, NEAR FORT LARAMIE, WYOMING

The stagecoach lurched and rolled its way across the arid landscape with sage and cactus poking through the sandy soil. The air inside the stage was thick with the odor of sweat and hair tonic. Emmie clutched the seat to keep from falling across the lap of the soldier sitting next to her. She still could hardly believe she was out here in the Great American Desert.

A grizzled soldier in the seat across from her leaned

forward and smiled a gap-toothed grin. His angular face was rough and reddened from the sun, and his uniform was none too clean. But he'd been friendly without being too familiar during the entire trip from Fort Leavenworth. "We'll get there today, miss."

Finally her new life was about to begin. "I'm ready to be off this stagecoach."

Catherine Courtney had given her a month to find other living arrangements, and surprisingly, the woman had been kind every time they met. After a flurry of telegrams and last-minute plans, Emmie had embarked on a train journey to a far-off place she'd only vaguely heard of. Now, ten days later, her journey was about to end. She bit her lip and tried to still the nervous pounding of her heart.

She peered out the open window. Dry buffalo grass, sage, and weeds undulated as far as she could see in every direction. She already missed the soft greens of Indiana. No towns or settlements, just endless plains of wilderness without much promise.

But there was no other option except the one offered by Mr. Eddingfield, and almost anything was better than that.

"Ever been West before, miss?" the soldier asked.

"Never." Emmie fanned her face and tried to keep her stomach from roiling at the stench of his breath mixed with the smell of rank, unwashed bodies and dusty leather in the tightly packed stagecoach.

"You ain't seen nothing until you seen them mountains out here. Lots of wide-open spaces."

The stage lurched again, and one of the soldiers up on top shouted, "Laramie up ahead!"

Emmie craned her head in a decidedly unladylike way out the window and tried to see, but the laboring horses threw up too much dust. She drew her head back in as the driver cursed at the flagging horses and urged them toward their destination. They stopped briefly at a swiftly running river, then the driver cracked the whip again and urged the team onto a waiting ferry. Her heart pounded as the fort grew nearer.

She pulled a handkerchief out of her reticule and wiped her face with it. She must look terrible. Her face and neck felt gritty with cinders from the train and her scalp itched. Large patches of dust and mud clung to her skirts and shoes. She tied her blue bonnet firmly under her chin as the driver pulled the team to a halt beside a crude adobe building. Soldiers milled around outside, and just across a wide parade ground, Emmie saw a neat row of whitewashed adobe buildings. This was the famous Fort Laramie? This assortment of rough buildings and barren wasteland? Her heart sank at the thought of living in this primitive place.

As she stepped off the stage, she gasped and almost fell when she caught sight of a throng of Indians outside the entrance to the building. Their buckskin clothing was in sharp contrast to the colorful blankets they had pulled around their shoulders. She tightened her grip on her cloak as a shield. She'd heard of all the Indian atrocities just a few months ago. The papers had called 1865 "the Bloody Year."

Her garrulous soldier friend chuckled at her small sound of dismay. "They won't hurt you none. Those Injuns are Laramie Loafers. They're too dependent on gov'ment rations to cause a peep of trouble."

She hesitantly followed the soldiers into the building. Inside even more Indians milled around. A counter made of rough wooden planks and piled with all kinds of necessities lined the back of the store, much like a general store back home. Barrels of sugar, flour, and tea sat off to one side, and wide shelves behind the counter held a wide assortment of items from coffee grinders and Arbuckle coffee to ribbons and beads and boots. The smell of coffee, dust, and sweat was almost overpowering. A single kerosene lamp swung from the ceiling, and its sickly glow cast a yellowish pall over everything.

Suddenly aware that the overwhelming babble had ceased and every eye was staring at her, Emmie flushed and forced herself to approach the sutler standing behind the counter. "Excuse me, sir, but could you tell me where I might find Lieutenant Rand Campbell?"

"That lucky lieutenant always has purty wimmenfolk lookin' for him." A scrawny soldier with bright red hair stepped up beside her before the sutler could answer. "I can take you to his wife, Miss Sarah." He thrust out a brown hand. "I'm Private Jackson Wheeler, but you can call me Rooster."

Emmie hesitated, then shook his hand gingerly. "I-I'm Emmie Croftner." She'd debated about what name to use and had decided on her legal one. She wanted to try to forget all about Monroe, if she could.

"Let's get out of this here crowd of buzzards. The lieutenant's little place is over yonder on the other side of the parade ground." Rooster opened the door for her and grabbed her satchel from her unresisting hand. "They'll be tickled pink to see you. You here to help with the wee one?"

"Yes." Emmie let the soldier ramble on. She was too tired to think or respond. She spared a glance around at her surroundings as she followed Rooster around the parade ground.

Soldiers stood in neat lines at attention as the trumpet blew a vaguely familiar tune. Two more soldiers lowered the flag from the flagpole in the middle of the field. Emmie felt a twinge of excitement and admiration at the rows of blue uniforms. There was something so masculine and attractive about a man in a uniform. Not that she was interested, of course. Between her shiftless brothers and her lying "husband," she'd had enough of men to last a lifetime. She just wanted a place to heal and a friend to talk to.

She couldn't help gawking as she followed Rooster's spry steps. A surprising amount of activity went on all around the fort. She could see a forest of tepees on the north side of the grounds, with Indian women stooping over campfires and half-naked children shouting and running between the tepees. Horses pranced around the stable on the far side of the field, and beyond that, the barren, sage-dotted landscape stretched right up to the edge of the purple mountains in the distance.

Rooster stopped outside a neat white bungalow with a wide front porch. He bounded up the steps and pounded on the first of two doors.

Sarah opened it with a squeal of delight and flung her arms around her. "Emmie! Oh, I'm so glad to see you. The stage must have been early—I intended to be there to meet you. Come in, come in." She motioned her in and waved her thanks at Rooster before she shut the door.

Emmie hadn't seen Sarah for nearly a year. Not since she had broken her engagement to Ben and followed Rand out here to this desolate place. Her bright golden hair still gleamed and her green eyes still sparkled with joy and excitement. She'd gained a little weight with her pregnancy, but the soft roundness suited Sarah's petite femininity.

"I'm chattering like a magpie, and you must be exhausted," Sarah said. "Would you like to freshen up while I fix us a cup of tea?"

"That would be lovely. I'm grimy from the trip." Emmie took off her bonnet and smiled at Sarah.

Sarah shuddered at the mention of the trip. "How well I remember the journey out here. Horrible food, no bathing facilities, no place to sleep. Why don't I heat some water for a bath? Rand won't be home until suppertime. You can have a lovely soak."

"Sounds heavenly. But I'll get it ready if you show me where everything is. Shouldn't you be resting?"

"Now you sound like Rand." Sarah laughed. "I feel wonderful. I have a ways to go—almost four months. It will be a long wait. I'm so anxious already."

Emmie followed her through the tiny quarters. The small entry led to a parlor about ten feet square. It was a homey room with an army cot, obviously used as a sofa, that was covered with a colorful Ohio Star quilt in burgundy-and-blue calico and matching pillows. Warm burgundy calico curtains and matching table covers topped with lace doilies added more color. A crude table and two chairs stood under the front window and held a Bible, a copy of Shakespeare's plays, *David Copperfield,* and *Wuthering Heights.* A mantel over the fireplace held a delicate rose tea set and several small china figurines.

Just off the parlor was a small kitchen. The rough table and chairs were painted the same warm burgundy as the curtains in the parlor. Pots hung from pegs along one wall, and a small cookstove occupied the middle of the room. A dry sink with a plank counter sat in one corner.

The door in the left wall of the kitchen opened into a tiny bedroom with only room for a bed and small chest. Sarah started to lift the hip bath from its peg on the wall, but Emmie quickly stepped forward and took it down herself. "I don't want to be a bother. I'm here to help you."

Sarah laughed as she pointed out a room in the corner for the bath. "I'll heat some water."

An hour later Emmie felt like a new woman. Her dark hair shone, and the lavender dress soothed her raw skin. They drank their tea and ate warm bread with thick butter and jam as they chatted. The months since they last talked seemed to fall away.

"Are you sure Rand is all right with my coming? Ben wouldn't be his favorite person."

A shadow passed through Sarah's eyes, but she smiled. "You aren't responsible for your brother's actions. Rand doesn't hold it against you. And he knew I needed some help. There are few women out here, and he is grateful you were willing to come."

Emmie's throat thickened. "You have no idea how

I needed a place to settle. I'll take good care of you, Sarah."

Sarah set down her teacup. "I was sorry to hear about your husband's death. You were married such a short time."

Emmie carefully chewed the last bit of her jam and bread before answering. She knew she needed to tell Sarah the truth, but she didn't think she could face it yet. She'd told her she wanted to take back her maiden name since she'd been married such a short time. But a secret of such magnitude never stayed hidden. Already a few people looked at her oddly in the last few days before she left Wabash.

Sarah patted her arm, her emerald eyes luminous with tears as she saw her friend's agitation. "We don't have to talk about it yet. Someday when the grief isn't so fresh and you want to tell me how wonderful Monroe was, I'll be ready to listen. It's still very difficult to talk about Papa. I still miss him so, and it's been almost a year." She dabbed at her eyes with a lace-trimmed handkerchief and quickly changed the subject.

Lieutenant Isaac Liddle brushed the crumbs left from lunch from his lap and grabbed his rifle. Chickadees fluttered from the trees to snatch up the bread crumbs. The *thunk* of axes on trees wafted through the forest. He and Rand were guarding the rest of the detail, but he felt relaxed. Things had been peaceful at Fort Laramie for weeks.

He eyed Rand's back. Things had been tense between them since Rand married Sarah, and Isaac had been waiting for the right time to talk to his friend. No time like the present. They were seldom alone, and there was always so much to do.

He cleared his throat. "Rand, I'd like to talk to you."

Rand Campbell, a broad-shouldered man in his midtwenties, turned from his perusal of the wild landscape. His dark brown eyes were cautious as they met Isaac's gaze. "Sure."

"It's time we cleared the air between us." Isaac took a step nearer and put his hand on Rand's shoulder. "I value your friendship, and I'd hate for a misunderstanding to come between us."

"You mean Sarah."

Isaac nodded and let go of Rand's shoulder. "Your

wife is a lovely girl. I was lonely and thought she might be too. But I was never in love with her. Not the way the two of you are. We might have made a decent match of it, but it never would have been what the two of you have. My heart isn't broken or anything even close to it."

Rand's gaze searched his, and he finally nodded. "I see that's true now. I thought maybe it was hard for you to be around us."

"What's hard is when you both avoid me at mess hall. Or look the other way at a dance. We were best friends. I still feel like you're my brother."

Rand held out his hand. "I'm glad you spoke up. I've missed you."

Isaac pumped Rand's hand. "Same here, friend."

"Sarah has a companion coming. Maybe the two of you will get along well."

Isaac released his grip and held up his hand. "Whoa there, buddy. Just because you're happily hitched doesn't mean the rest of us want to follow in your footsteps."

Rand waggled his brows. "She's a pretty one."

Isaac grinned. "No thanks."

His step was lighter as he led his horse to the river to drink. At least things were square between his buddy and him.

Emmie sat at the table peeling potatoes for supper. The delicious aroma of venison stew filled the kitchen. Being with Sarah had healed a bit of the pain she carried.

"I'm starving, wife," Rand called as he strode into the kitchen followed by Sarah's younger brother.

Emmie wiped her hands on her apron and stood. "Joel, you've grown a foot."

He grinned. "I can shoot now too." His glance at Rand held adoration.

The nine-year-old boy had a confidence that sharpened his expression and squared his shoulders. Rand's influence had been good for Joel, who had seen little approval from Wade, their older brother.

Rand exuded a quiet strength and compassion. The dimples in his cheeks made her want to smile with him. How would he treat the sister of his archrival?

But her fears were groundless. Rand was the perfect host and asked her for news of home as Sarah put the venison stew on the table.

"Usually we go to officers' mess," Sarah said. "But I didn't want to share you with the men your first night here. They'll be around soon enough when they hear there's a young, beautiful widow in their midst."

Rand grinned. "They already know. I had at least ten men ask me about her. I had to tell them I hadn't seen her for over six months and she might be an ugly hag by now. I can see I was mistaken."

Emmie flushed. "I'm not interested in finding another husband. Not ever." Any mention of her looks always made her uncomfortable. She knew she was very ordinary. Only Monroe had ever called her beautiful, and it was obvious now that he'd lied. Her real attraction for him had been the dowry that never materialized.

Rand raised his eyebrows but said nothing. After supper Emmie and Sarah cleared the table and washed the dishes, then followed him into the tiny parlor. He took down two harmonicas, handed one to Joel, and they began to play "Nearer, My God to Thee," as Sarah sang the words in a clear, sweet soprano.

Emmie knew the song a bit. It was one her father bellowed when he was drunk. So after a slight hesitation, she joined in with an alto harmony.

Sarah clapped her hands. "That was wonderful. We like to have devotions together at night. We sing and Rand reads a passage of Scripture. Would you like to join us, or are you too tired tonight?"

"I'd love to join you." Something about their simple, heartfelt faith pulled her. She'd always felt that God was too busy to pay any attention to someone like her. But Sarah and Rand acted as if he were right there with them.

Rand picked up the worn Bible on the table by the window and flipped through the pages. "We're up to Psalms," he said, settling his broad-shouldered frame into the chair. He began to read Psalm 61 in his deep voice. "'Hear my cry, O God; attend unto my prayer. From the end of the earth will I cry unto thee, when my heart is overwhelmed: lead me to the rock that is higher than I. For thou hast been a shelter for me, and a strong tower from the enemy.'" His voice faltered and fell silent as the tears slid noiselessly down Emmie's cheeks.

"No, no, go on," she choked. "It's what I need to hear."

As he finished the psalm, she felt a curious peace. This place was certainly the ends of the earth like the Scripture mentioned, so maybe she would find answers here.

FOUR

The shrill notes of the bugle pierced the dawn air, and Emmie bolted upright in the narrow bed Rand and Sarah had fixed her in the hallway. Without sliding out of the cot, she looked out the window in the top of the door. Streaks of pink heralding the day lightened the dark sky. She slid out of bed, shivering as her bare feet touched the cold floor, and padded to the door. The sound of men grooming their horses drifted across the parade ground. She pushed open the door and took a deep breath of sage scented air.

She was here at Fort Laramie, that famous bastion of might against the hordes of savages threatening the settlers trekking along the Oregon Trail. Or so the men back home said. She herself hadn't seen any threatening hordes in the short time she'd been here, just those Laramie Loafers. But there were certainly a lot of impressive-looking soldiers.

She shut the door and watched through the window. The two-story barracks across the parade ground bustled with blue-coated men hurrying toward the mess hall for their breakfast, then on to saddle their horses or start their fatigue duties of the day.

She poured water from the tin pitcher into the cracked bowl sitting on a cloth-covered crate. She shivered as the cold water hit her neck and face. Pulling on a simple blue cotton dress, she braided her long dark hair and coiled it around her head. By the time she finished her ablutions, she could hear Rand and Sarah moving around the kitchen.

"Good morning," Sarah said as Emmie came toward her with a smile. "Did you sleep well?"

"I woke up a few times when somebody kept yelling 'All's well.'"

Sarah and Rand chuckled.

"Night watchman. You'll get used to it," Rand told her. He kissed Sarah and picked up his hat. "I'm going to be late for boots and saddles if I don't get a move on."

"Boots and saddles? What's that—some kind of war game?"

Rand grinned at the question. "That's the call to mount our horses and get on with our day. I've got to lead a detail to escort a wagon train coming in and then round up some beef for Cookie—that's what the cook's called at any fort I've ever been at. But I'll wager the men will be finding any excuse to come over here to meet you."

Rand's prediction proved true. Nearly every man in the fort made some excuse to drop in over the next few days. Emmie felt conspicuous even going outside for a walk or to the sutler's store. Men stared at her with awe and something like deep respect in their eyes. It was very intimidating, especially when she felt as she did about all males. Except for Rand. He was a very nice man, God-fearing, and honest to a fault. But there couldn't be two like him in the world.

Each soldier showed up hat in hand, hair slicked back with a hair tonic that smelled of spice, blue uniform brushed and pressed. Emmie felt sorry for them, but she let Sarah deal with sending them away. Two even proposed marriage, practically in their first breaths.

"I just can't stay inside another minute," Sarah announced one day after sending Joel off to school. "I'm not used to having to sit around here all day. I don't know why the doctor said I couldn't continue to teach the Sioux children. I feel fine."

"He's just being cautious." Rand shoveled the last bite of flapjacks into his mouth. "How about a picnic? The weather has been warm, but it won't last long. You might as well enjoy it while you can."

Sarah's eyes brightened. "I love that idea. How about you, Emmie?"

Though the thought of leaving the safety of the fort took her aback, Emmie nodded. "That would be wonderful." She'd come here to be of help to Sarah, and she couldn't let a little fear stand in her way.

Rand pulled on his coat. "I'd go with you, but I need to repair some telegraph line the Indians cut. I'll arrange for an escort. What time do you want to go?"

"Could we go to the stream in the meadow?"

"Sure. Just don't wander off."

"Thank you, Rand." Sarah leaned up to brush a quick kiss over his lips.

The sight made Emmie's chest squeeze, and she turned away. It would be hard to ever trust a man with her heart again. Not after such betrayal.

After their morning chores, the women took the laundry to Soapsuds Row, a line of tents at the edge of the fort where a couple of enlisted men lived with their wives, who acted as the fort laundresses. The women were visiting back East right now and the men did the laundry while they were gone. Sarah and Emmie hurried back to their quarters and packed lunch.

Promptly at eleven, someone pounded on the door and called in a deep baritone, "I'm here to escort you."

Emmie swung open the door and looked up into the bluest eyes she'd ever seen. The man had a friendly, open face with a shock of auburn hair that fell down over his forehead from under his blue hat. His flowing mustache matched his hair and he was quite tall, for she had to crane her neck to look up at him. At least six-two, his stocky frame towered over her.

He took off his hat and held it in his big hands,

reddened from the wind. "You must be Emmie. Every man in the fort is already in love with you."

Emmie smiled in spite of her resolve to keep aloof from the soldiers. His grin was infectious. "They just haven't seen any women in a while. And who are you?"

"Isaac Liddle at your service, ma'am." He slapped the heels of his boots together and kissed her hand, then grinned again at her surprise.

She tried to place his soft accent. "I've heard a lot about you. You're Rand's buddy."

Sarah joined her at the door. "I see you've met Mr. Liddle. You behave yourself, Isaac. I don't want you scaring Emmie into leaving me."

His voice took on an injured tone. "Now, Sarah, that's ridiculous. One look at my handsome mug and she's sure to want to stay. Besides, I'm here to escort you two on your picnic. Every man in the fort clamored for the job, but I know how to get around your husband. All I had to do was promise to shine his boots for the next six months."

Something about his laughing manner made Emmie's shields go up. Monroe had been lighthearted and carefree too. The facade had hidden his true heart of irresponsibility and falsehoods. Rand and

Sarah might like Isaac, but Emmie wasn't about to be betrayed again by smiling eyes.

"Come right this way, ladies. Your steeds await you."

Sarah laughed as he took the picnic basket from her, but Emmie pressed her lips together and turned her gaze away.

Isaac couldn't keep his gaze from straying to Emmie. Her hair was as black and glossy as a raven's wing, and the vulnerability in her haunted blue eyes tugged at him. Someone had hurt her, and the thought made him clench his fists.

He led the buckskin mare to her side. "Molly's a darling, aren't you, girl? Look at her gentle eyes." Isaac patted the insistent nose the mare thrust into his hand. "Have you ridden much, Miss Croftner?"

"Not really, but I like horses." She tentatively held out her palm, and the mare snuffled her velvet nose against it. "We had a pony when I was little. He was an old pinto and ornery."

"Well, Molly will be good for you. She's gentle and sweet-natured."

"You sound as though you know a lot about horses."

"A fair bit. My family raised racehorses."

He offered his linked hands to help her mount the mare. After a moment's hesitation, Emmie stepped into his hands, and he helped her up onto the side-saddle. She adjusted her skirts and gathered the reins as he helped Sarah. Her friend's horse was a placid bay with a wide back.

Rand had given him explicit instructions on making sure the horse he picked for Sarah wouldn't bolt or throw her off in her delicate condition.

Isaac led the way past the parade ground and the stables where four other soldiers joined them. As they crossed in front of the Sioux encampment, he moved his horse to fall in with Emmie's. He watched her eyes widen at the sight of the women and children. She wrinkled her nose at the pungent scent of some concoction bubbling in the pot over the open fire they skirted, mingled with dung from the numerous dogs roaming the fort area. Sarah waved and called to several Indian women.

The sun blazed down in the brilliant blue canopy of sky. Fluffy white clouds drifted across the banner above them like lazy puffs of smoke. A bird cried out and Isaac looked up to see an eagle soar into the brilliant haze above them.

Emmie looked too. "Is that an eagle?"

"Sure is."

She gave a sigh, and a contented smile lurked around her mouth. "This West is a wonderful place. It feels so free here."

"You don't mind the primitive conditions?"

She shook her head. "I've lived with better and I've lived with worse. I've found that my surroundings aren't a good prediction of happiness."

He eyed her shuttered expression. Something had caused her pain. She'd make a good wife to a soldier. He dragged his gaze away from her entrancing face. "You're riding well."

She patted Molly's neck. "She's made it easy. How did you happen to join the cavalry instead of staying back with your family raising horses?"

"I'm the youngest of four brothers. They had no need of my help." And his eldest brother had made it clear there was no room for Isaac on the ranch. Not after he'd let their prize mare die birthing. "But there is much opportunity here. I'm going to run cattle in a few years."

She shuddered. "It seems so dangerous out here."

"It won't be for long. Settlers are pouring in. You'll see."

They stopped by a cold, clear stream running through a meadow. The scent of sage hung in the air, and Isaac pointed out a prickly pear cactus for them to avoid stepping in as they dismounted and followed him to a shady spot under a cottonwood tree beside the stream.

Emmie spread a blanket on the mossy ground by the stream. "It's lovely."

Isaac straightened the other side of the blanket and sat down while she and Sarah opened the hamper of food. "It'll be even more beautiful in the spring. There will be bluebells and violets everywhere."

The four privates each took a separate spot in different directions and stood watch for hostile Sioux. Sarah and Emmie took them a plate of food before settling down on the blanket with Isaac.

He watched Emmie's face surreptitiously as they ate their lunch of cold sandwiches and baked beans. Did she know he'd once courted Sarah? He glanced from Sarah to Emmie and realized once again that he'd just been lonely when he'd been calling on Sarah.

Something about Emmie spoke to him at a deeper level. Her vulnerability drew him.

He wasn't sure he was ready for an emotion that powerful.

FIVE

⟨≈⟩

Emmie soon fell into the pattern of fort life, listening almost unconsciously for the trumpet to sound out the various calls. She didn't need the little watch pinned to her bodice anymore. Her days were divided by reveille at 5:00 a.m., breakfast at 6:00, followed by stable call at 6:30, drill at 10:00 and 2:00, retreat at 6:00 p.m., tattoo at 8:30, and taps at 8:45. She loved to watch the boots and saddles call in the morning. At the order, the cavalry swung up into their saddles in unison, the sun dancing off their brass buttons and their sabers. Then they would ride out of the fort grounds onto the open plain to practice wheeling and charging imaginary foes. It was an exhilarating sight.

After she'd been there a month and was finally beginning to settle in and feel at home, Rand came bursting in and sat in a chair beside them. "I received new orders today."

Sarah stopped eating the dumplings made with dried apples and put her fork down. "Oh no, Rand. Where? I don't want to go anywhere else."

His grin widened at the dismay in her voice. "We're going to Fort Phil Kearny."

Sarah shrieked and jumped to throw her arms around him. He almost toppled backward in his chair. "I get to see Amelia!" she cried as she hugged him exuberantly.

He sat the chair forward with a thump. "I thought you didn't want to go."

Emmie watched with a pensive smile. If she could have a marriage like her friend, she might consider it, but there weren't very many men like Rand Campbell around. She pushed away the stirring of envy. What made her think she even deserved such a fine man?

Emmie knew Amelia McCallister, of course. She was the daughter of Wabash's only doctor. It was the talk of the whole town when Amelia married Jacob Campbell and moved out West with him. Sarah spoke often of how much she missed her best friend, and Emmie couldn't help a stab of jealousy. Would Sarah have time for her once Amelia was around?

"When do we leave?" Emmie asked.

"You've both got two days to pack."

Sarah frowned. "Two days! You must be joking."

"They wanted me to go tomorrow, but I talked the colonel into another day in deference to you ladies. And that's quite a feat with the army. They usually don't officially recognize that the wives exist. In the army's eyes you two are just camp followers like the ones across the river."

Emmie grew hot at his oblique reference to the soiled doves on the other side of the Laramie River. Would he put her in the same class as the prostitutes if he knew about her false marriage? She hoped she never had to find out. Her resolve to tell Sarah the truth had faded as the days passed. Why risk seeing her friend's love and respect change to repugnance?

By working late both nights, they managed to get

everything packed. Rand brought them empty pickle barrels, and they packed most of their belongings in the pungent barrels with hay packed around the breakables.

Joel scooted a barrel toward the door. "I can't wait to see Jimmy again! I bet he knows I'm coming. Maybe he even asked his dad to arrange it." He glanced at Emmie. "His dad is the post commander. So maybe I helped get us back together with Jacob and Amelia."

His sister chuckled. "So I have you to thank for all this packing?"

Uncertainty darkened his eyes. "Aren't you glad you get to see Amelia?"

Sarah ruffled his blond hair. "Very excited. So thank you."

His smile broadened. "You're welcome."

Both women were almost sick with excitement and nerves as they pulled out of the fort two days later. Emmie was curious to see something of the countryside. She'd already begun to chafe at the restrictions on her movements in the fort. In thirty-five days she'd only been out of the confines of the fort once on that picnic to the meadow.

They boarded the ambulance, a heavy wagon

outfitted with a straw mattress and canvas sides rolled up to let the breeze in. A canteen hung near the roof with the lid off to allow the water to cool in the breeze. Rand had rigged up a padded bench seat along each side for them to ride on, and the rest of their belongings were packed into every available inch of space. By the time they'd gone a mile, both women wished they had a horse to ride. The ambulance had no springs, and they were jarred and thrown about with every pothole as they moved with the troop of forty men.

They stopped for lunch and the women got down. Emmie drew deep breaths of sage-scented air as she bolted down the beans and bacon the cook presented. The bacon was tough so she ate around it.

"I wish there was such a thing as a portable privy," Sarah whispered. "Can you bring the blanket and come with me?"

The women hurried off a short distance on the far side of a scraggly cottonwood tree, and Emmie held the blanket up as a screen. Above their heads the branches swayed with the breeze, and Emmie caught a whiff of some sweetly scented autumn wildflower. The gurgle of the clear creek to their right muted the sounds of the army camp behind them.

"That's one bad thing about being pregnant," Sarah said. "You can't wait very long. I don't know how I'd manage without another woman along." She hurriedly rearranged her skirts, then took her turn holding the blanket for Emmie.

"Hurry," she said. "I think they're about ready to go, and I don't think they saw us leave."

By the time they started back, the ambulance was pulling away without them in it. They ran, shouting for the soldiers to stop. Rand saw them and halted the procession.

His gaze darted over Sarah's shoulder into the woods as he took her arm and helped her to the ambulance. "Don't ever go off like that again without telling me. We never know when we're going to run into hostiles this far from the fort." His lips flattened, and he glowered at both of them. "You know what happened last time."

Sarah flushed and tossed her head. "It didn't turn out so bad. I made some new friends."

"And almost got killed, and Jacob too." His glare softened. "Sorry, Green Eyes, but you scared me half to death. Please, let me know next time, okay?"

Sarah looked contrite. "You're right. I should have told you. I will next time."

"What's he talking about?" Emmie was shocked at the ruckus their little necessary errand had caused.

Sarah sighed, then picked up the knitting she'd been working on before lunch. The little yellow booties she was making were half finished. "I went off by myself on a ride and Indians took me. But they weren't warriors, just Laramie Loafers, and it wouldn't have happened if your brother hadn't put them up to it."

"Ben? You've seen him? Why didn't you tell me before this?"

Sarah stopped a moment, then sighed and went on. "The Sioux left me in a cabin for Ben, but I got away from him and some hostile Sioux found me. Little Wolverine was a young Sioux who respected Rand because of an earlier battle, and he protected me until Rand found me." She shook her head and sighed again. "Jacob was injured by a bear while they were out searching for me. So now, Rand keeps a close watch on me."

Emmie could tell her friend was uncomfortable talking about Ben, but this was as good a time as any to clear the air. The entire time since she'd arrived, she knew they both had been avoiding the subject of her brother. She noticed Sarah's downcast expression. "I don't have any illusions about my brother's character, Sarah. I lived with him, remember?"

Sarah took a deep breath. "That's not all, Emmie. There's something I've put off telling you. I didn't want to hurt you after you'd been through so much."

Emmie's stomach tightened. "What is it?"

"Ben was killed in a fall from his horse while fleeing the Sioux. Labe told Rand."

Emmie looked down at her hands, then back at Sarah. She wasn't sure how she felt about Ben, but she cared about Labe. He'd been good to her in his clumsy way. "Is Labe all right?"

Sarah nodded. "He joined up with a group of miners passing through here a couple of months ago. They were headed up the Bozeman Trail to the goldfields in Montana."

So much death. Everywhere she looked there was death. First Monroe and now Ben. She had no idea how she came to be there, but she suddenly found herself sobbing against Sarah's shoulder. She didn't know why she was crying. She'd never been close to Ben, but he was her older brother, and now that he was gone, she was even more alone in the world. She'd probably never see Labe again either.

By evening the wind picked up and began to moan through overhanging rocks. Black thunderheads rolled in over the tops of the bluffs and jagged flashes of lightning lit the roiling undersides.

"Get the horses tied down, and check on the cattle," Isaac shouted after the supply train went into corral formation. His gaze went to the ambulance conveying the women. They'd be frightened. He urged his horse in that direction.

The wind struck with a fearful punch and caught at the canvas of the ambulance. He saw Emmie struggling to unroll one side of the canvas while Sarah fought with the other side. After quickly dismounting, Isaac leaped to help them. Needles of cold rain pierced him as he grabbed hold of the wet fabric.

"Are you all right?" he shouted above the thunder and rain.

Emmie pushed the heavy wet hair out of her face and nodded. Looming out of the driving rain, Rand dashed to secure the canvas on Sarah's side.

"Isaac," Emmie gasped. "Where did you come from? I thought you stayed behind in Fort Laramie."

He tied the canvas back with the rope and grinned at her. "I've been on ahead scouting. You didn't think I would let a pretty gal like you get away, did you?"

Even with her hair plastered to her head and her dress covered with mud, he'd never seen a prettier sight. He patted her head and turned to tend to the frightened cattle.

Emmie pulled her shawl around her protectively. He'd patted her like—like she was a dog or a child. Was that how he saw her? She pushed away the prick of hurt and climbed back into the ambulance.

The storm cleared quickly and the procession moved on. Emmie found her eyes straying more often than she liked to Isaac's erect figure on the bay gelding. His burnished hair curled over his collar, and he was easy to pick out of the group. He seemed to have a kind and encouraging word for everyone. All the more reason for her not to believe him when he said she was beautiful. He was evidently one of those people who looked for the good in everyone. An admirable quality, she had to admit, but it made her more cautious.

"You ready to go back to Indiana?" Sarah asked when they took a short break in the middle of the afternoon.

"I thought about it," Emmie admitted. "This wilderness is a fearful place. Even the storms are wilder." Then she smiled. "But it is beautiful in a wild and savage way. I love the scent of sage in the wind and the deep, rich reds and browns of the earth. And I can't wait to get a closer look at the mountains."

They saw wildlife everywhere. Elk, deer, jackrabbit, and once a small herd of buffalo off in the distance. Emmie wanted to get a closer look at the famous beast, but they hadn't come close enough to see well.

"That's why the Indians are so set on keeping this area," Sarah told her when she mentioned the abundant game. "And since the Montana gold mines opened up and miners keep traipsing through on the Bozeman Trail, the game is beginning to thin out. Red Cloud is said to be gathering a large war band up in the Powder River area. He's promised a fight to the knife. Rand doesn't know where it will all end. He sees the Indians' point of view, but he knows we have to expand clear to the Pacific if this nation is going to thrive. We need the railroad completed and the telegraph to all cities. The Indians won't stand by and see it happen without a fight." She shivered. "It scares me when I think about it. Every time Rand goes out on detail, I'm terrified he won't come back."

Emmie hadn't realized it was so dangerous. So far she hadn't seen a single hostile Indian. It was hard to imagine that the problem was as severe as Sarah said.

Rand called a halt around six o'clock. After beating the brush for rattlesnakes, three men pitched a tepee-like structure called a Sibley tent for the ladies.

"What are you doing?" Emmie asked Rooster as he uncoiled a large horsehair rope.

"Snakes won't cross a horsehair rope." He laid it on the ground all around the tent and bedrolls. "Reckon they don't like them hairs ticklin' their bellies. Rattlers ain't nothin' to mess with, and we don't want to lose our only wimmenfolk. 'Course it's late in the year for snakes, but it's so much warmer than usual, I don't 'tend to take any chances."

Emmie wasn't sure if he was telling the truth, but his words sounded comforting, so she and Sarah carried their clothes and blankets inside and tried to make the interior comfortable. When they came out of the tent, one of the men had gotten a blazing fire going. The aroma of stew made Emmie's mouth water. She had hardly touched her lunch, but now she was famished. She ate two plates of the delicious stew and washed it down with the water in the battered tin cup Rooster gave her.

While four of the men went off to stand guard duty after supper, Rand brought out the harmonicas. The plaintive notes of "Home Sweet Home" mingled with the crackle of the fire and the howl of some animal in the hills to their left.

Joel nestled close to his sister's side. "Jimmy doesn't know how to play the harmonica, I bet."

"What's that?" Emmie knew her voice was too shrill when several of the soldiers snickered and Joel grinned.

"It's just a pack of coyotes," Isaac said. "They're more scared of you than you are of them."

Emmie shivered at another howl. "I wouldn't be too sure of that," she said shakily.

Rand played a couple of hymns and the men joined in song. Rooster had a surprisingly deep bass voice and Isaac sang tenor. But it had been a long day on the trail and they were all yawning, so Rand sent them all off to find their bedrolls.

Isaac stood waiting for them by the ambulance. "I'll be right outside if you need anything." His gaze lingered on Emmie.

She let him escort her to the tent, and her pulse leapt at the press of his warm fingers on her arm. It meant nothing though—only that she missed a man's touch.

SIX

The landscape grew more wild and untamed as the procession turned north and trekked up toward Fort Phil Kearny, and Isaac kept a sharp gaze on the hills. No telling if Sioux watched them even now.

The mountains loomed in the distance, their purple peaks blending into the deep azure sky. Game flourished everywhere, and Isaac and his men had no trouble providing fresh meat to supplement the mess-chest fare. The rest of the section he ordered to keep close together as they all kept a sharp lookout for Indians.

E. B. Taylor had attempted to negotiate a constructive peace treaty in May 1866, but Red Cloud had angrily stomped out when Colonel Carrington showed up to establish three new forts in the last of the Sioux hunting grounds. Red Cloud objected that the army would be setting up forts without waiting for the agreement from the Indians to allow troops to patrol the Bozeman Trail.

These past months had been tense, with numerous skirmishes between soldiers and Indians. Red Cloud was said to be massing together not just Sioux but Cheyenne and Arapaho to fight the invasion of bluecoats. Along this very trail just a month earlier, three soldiers had been killed and several others wounded during an ambush. So Isaac preached constant vigilance and caution.

The nights were cool and clear. Once he pointed out a pack of timber wolves on a bluff overlooking the camp. He assured the women they were safe from attack, but Emmie had spent the rest of the evening with her haunted gaze on the hills. The journey was taking its toll on both women, and he saw how Rand watched his wife with a growing worry. They'd been on the trail for eight days, and safety was still another two days away.

Isaac came back from a hunting trip to find Emmie waiting for him. "Isaac, have you noticed how poorly Sarah looks?"

He nodded, his brow crinkling with worry. "There's a post surgeon at Fort Phil Kearny who can take a look at her. It's only another three days or so away. I've been thinking we might camp here an extra day. The horses could do with the rest too."

Emmie's brow furrowed. "I think that's too long. She needs a break now. Could we stop for an extra night?"

He paused and looked out over the landscape. "We're in a good location to see any approaching attack. I can talk to Rand about it. Every day we're out here the danger escalates though."

"I know we all want to get to the safety of the fort, but I don't want Sarah to lose the baby."

He let his gaze linger on her. She was pale too, and some tendrils of dark hair had come loose from the pins. His fingers itched to touch one of the silky curls hanging in her face. Her concern for Sarah touched him too.

Emmie didn't seem to notice his rapt gaze. "She keeps pushing herself so. Today is the first time she's agreed to take a nap. And with the river right here, maybe we could clean up too."

Isaac nodded slowly. "I'll post extra sentries and string up some blankets for privacy. I could use a bath and a shave myself." He rubbed his grizzled cheeks with a rueful grin and watched her almost skip away to tell Sarah.

Emmie was beginning to despise that ambulance. She lifted her skirt off the ground and climbed into the canvas wagon. Sarah was braiding her long red-gold hair when Emmie shut the flap behind her.

Sarah looked a little brighter. "I've been asleep for over two hours."

"You needed it. And I have exciting news." Emmie sat next to Sarah. "We're going to stop beside the creek for an extra day to rest up and bathe."

Sarah brightened immediately, a little pink rushing to her pale cheeks. "Oh, lovely. I was just feeling sorry for myself before you came. Missing Wabash and my father." She stood up as she thrust the last pin into place. "I'm so glad you're here, Emmie. I could not have endured this trip alone."

Emmie laughed self-consciously. "I'm just grateful

I had somewhere to go when Monroe was killed." As she hugged her friend, she tried to push away the guilt she felt over not being completely honest. Someday the truth would have to be told, but not now.

The afternoon sun still blazed by the time they wandered down to the stream to find Rand, but the air was brisk. True to his word, Isaac had rigged up a rope with blankets around a lovely pool of water. It looked clear and inviting, and Emmie couldn't wait to strip off her clothes and plunge in.

"I'll go get us some clean clothes," she told Sarah.

By the time she got back, Sarah had pulled off her shoes and stockings. She sat with her skirt pulled up to her knees and her feet dangling in the water. Emmie looked all around, but the soldiers were busy about their other duties setting up camp.

Joel was by the privacy screen. "I'll stand guard." His youthful voice held resolve.

"The very guard I'd choose." Reassured of their privacy, she slipped behind the curtain and pulled off her stained and dusty dress and the pins from her hair. She plunged in and came up sputtering. "It's like ice," she gasped. The cold seeped into her bones.

Sarah wasted no time in joining her. Birds chirped

in the trees around them and the breeze lapped the water into gentle waves and ripples as they quickly washed their hair. The water was too cold to stay in long, and the cool breeze chilled their damp skin.

After they dressed, they left their hair down to dry as they washed their dirty clothes. Sarah looked better already. Emmie spread their wet clothes out on the rocks and sat at the edge of the stream. She sighed, a sound of pure enjoyment as she felt the heat from the rock she was sitting on radiate warmth through her chilled body.

Almost dozing, she stretched out in the sun like a cat until a faint movement on the other side of the stream about fifty yards away caught her eye. "Oh, Sarah, look! Is that a buffalo?"

Sarah squinted against the glare of the sun as the movement came again. "Indians!" she screamed as she jumped to her feet.

Aware they'd been seen, the dim shapes rose to their feet and threw off their buffalo robes. Charging across the shallow creek with fierce yells, they headed straight toward the women with their tomahawks raised over their heads.

"Injuns!" Joel whipped away the privacy screen.

He dropped to one knee and aimed his rifle at the Sioux. "Run to the ambulance!"

A shot rang out from his gun, and Emmie saw the closest warrior fall facedown into the water.

She grabbed Sarah's hand and dragged her toward the ambulance as she screamed for Rand. Sarah shouted for Joel to run with him, and she grabbed his arm as they reached him.

He shook off her grip. "Leave me be, Sarah. I'm not a kid." He took aim again.

Before Sarah could insist he leave with them, Isaac and Rand, followed by four or five other soldiers, charged toward the Indians.

Rand aimed his gun. "Run! I'll take care of Joel."

Emmie nodded and propelled Sarah toward the circled wagons. Only after several steps did she realize Isaac was on Sarah's other side, helping her hurry. Shots rang out, and Emmie dared a glance back. The fierce expressions the Sioux wore made her put on a bigger spurt of speed.

Isaac dropped to one knee and aimed his rifle toward the advancing Indians. "Get under the wagon."

A fearsomely painted warrior choked and fell seconds after the rifle cracked. Soldiers raced from all over the camp to join the fray. Emmie covered her ears at the booming gunfire and the terrifying screams and shouts. She was sure she and Sarah were about to die.

Rooster rolled in under the wagon beside the women. "Don't you fear, missy," he panted to Emmie. "No Injun's gonna git ya. I'll shoot ya first myself 'fore I let them red devils take ya."

Shoot them himself? Emmie swallowed hard. Was being captured by Indians that bad?

Unaware of the shock his words caused Emmie, Rooster fired his rifle methodically at the faltering horde of Sioux. A few minutes later it was over. One man was dead and three were injured, including Rand, who had taken an arrow in the left arm.

Joel strutted around the camp with his chest puffed out. "Wait until Jimmy hears I shot three of them."

"You were a good guard," Emmie told him as she watched Sarah fuss over Rand.

"It's just a scratch," Rand said. "I'm all right, Green Eyes." He held her with his good arm as she burst into tears, then he saw Emmie's face and held out his bleeding arm for her to join them.

She buried her face against the other side of his

shirt for just a moment. Once she gathered her composure, she pulled away.

Isaac's vivid blue eyes met Emmie's, and she had to check the impulse to run to him. Turning away from his anxious gaze, she pulled out of Rand's protective clasp so Sarah could tend to his wound. Emmie hurried toward the tent before she disgraced herself by begging Isaac to hold her. What was wrong with her anyway that she would have such a crazy thought? Men couldn't be trusted. She'd best not let herself forget that.

Three hours later Emmie was still too keyed up to sleep. She could hear Rand's rhythmic breathing on the other side of the tent. Sarah snuffled occasionally in her sleep as she lay enfolded in his good arm with Joel on the other side. She'd wanted to make sure both the males in her life were within arm's reach.

Emmie shivered as she rolled over on her back and sat up. Maybe she'd just go out and sit by the fire for a while. The cold wouldn't leave her bones.

Rooster looked up as she lifted the flap on the

tent and slipped outside. "Howdy, Miz Emmie. Can't sleep?"

She shook her head. "I've never been so frightened in my life, Rooster." She settled down beside him as he rummaged through his haversack and handed her a piece of jerky.

"Here. Jaw on this awhile. It'll wear you out."

She smiled as she took the jerky. "Did you mean what you said about shooting us yourself?"

"'Course I meant it. It's the unwritten law out here. We don't never want to let our wimmenfolk fall into the hands of them red devils. We know what they do to 'em. We been told to save a bullet for any female and one for ourselves."

Emmie shuddered. "What do they do to women?"

"No use in you knowin', 'cause it ain't goin' to happen to you." He avoided her eyes as he poked the fire with a stick.

"But what if it did?" She always preferred to know the worst. The things she imagined were always worse than the reality, so it was better to just know and set her mind at rest. Being killed by Indians couldn't be any worse in reality than it was in her imagination.

But Rooster just clamped his jaw tight. "Don't go

coaxin' me to tell you 'cause I ain't gonna do it. Old Rooster ain't never goin' to let them git you, so don't you bother yer purty head about it."

And that's all he would say, so Emmie had to be content with the horrors of her imagination. She could tell he meant what he said about shooting her first. And that scared her. What if one of the soldiers shot them because they thought they'd be captured and help arrived just in the nick of time? She shivered. Maybe she should ask Rand to change the rule. She yawned, finally sleepy, and mumbling good night to Rooster, made her way back to her tent.

Isaac stood in the stirrups to stretch his muscles as the sunrise cast golden rays across their path. He had awakened the wagon train early and was even more eager to reach the safe haven of the fort after the ambush two days before.

The women had rolled up the sides of the ambulance so they could watch the approach to Fort Phil Kearny.

Isaac pointed out the majestic peaks in the

distance. "That's the Bighorn Mountains. Beautiful, aren't they? This Powder River country is the last of the Sioux hunting grounds. It's usually thick with buffalo, but they're beginning to thin out from the white man hunting them. The Indians are afraid that if they let us establish the Bozeman Trail along here, we'll drive away the last of the game. And they're right, as usual. It's already starting to happen."

"Maybe that's a good thing," Emmie said. "With no game, they'll go somewhere else."

Sarah frowned. "I lived with the Sioux for a short while. It was a curiously peaceful life where we worked for our food and really lacked nothing important. Their ways aren't any different to us than our ways are to the Europeans. The Indian women do beautiful needlework. Sometime I'll show you my buckskin dress and take you to see inside a Sioux tepee. My friend White Dove taught me a lot about what's really important in life. Things like love and unity and self-sufficiency. You would like her."

"Where is she now?" Emmie asked.

When Sarah glanced at him, Isaac realized she didn't know. Maybe Rand had tried not to worry her. "She's with Little Wolverine in Red Cloud's resistance, as far as I know. Rand and I tried to talk them out of going, but they said they had to stand with their people before the Sioux are no more."

Emmie shivered and tugged the blanket more tightly around her legs. "How can Rand fight the Indians when he has friends among them? What if Little Wolverine was with the band who attacked us?"

Isaac glanced at the hills around them. Danger could be anywhere, and he'd expected an attack on the route. "It would be Rand's worst nightmare to have to fight his friend. I don't know if he could or not."

If only his own brothers had Rand's integrity.

SEVEN

"Phil Kearny ahead!" Rand called.

Sarah and Emmie both thrust their heads out under the rolled-up canvas on the sides of the wagon and looked eagerly for their destination. Emmie could see sentries on a hill ahead waving signal flags.

"They're signaling our arrival to the fort," Sarah told her. "The commander will send out an escort."

Rand had ordered the women to stay in the ambulance away from the possible eyes of hostiles, but Emmie longed to climb out of the lurching conveyance and run on ahead to the fort. The thought of sleeping in a real bed was enticing. As she and Sarah looked toward the fort, a wagon loaded with wood lumbered by. On the back of the wagon a bloodstained figure lolled, one arm flung down the back of the wagon. Emmie thought he looked like he had red hair like Isaac until Sarah gasped.

"That soldier's been scalped," Sarah choked out, her hand to her mouth.

Emmie shuddered and looked around fearfully for the Indians who had committed the atrocity. But the wooded hills around the fort looked peaceful. The ambulance jerked forward as the driver urged the horses to a trot. Rand had seen the dead soldier and motioned the troops to hurry toward the safety of the fort.

As they pulled inside the stockaded garrison, soldiers milled around shouting orders. "Do you see Amelia?" Sarah asked anxiously.

Emmie looked around but saw no other women. She consulted the gold watch pinned to her dress. "It's around lunchtime. Maybe we could find her in the mess hall."

They climbed down out of the ambulance and Emmie staggered, a little unsteady on her feet, as though the ground were lurching under her. "It looks more like I thought Laramie would look. There are stockades and sentries along the blockhouses."

Sarah nodded. "If that murdered soldier is anything to go by, they need all the protection they can get. There's no telegraph line strung this far north, so if they've been having a lot of trouble with hostiles, they wouldn't be able to wire for reinforcements." Joel was dancing around impatiently, so she gave him permission to go look for his friend.

Rand stepped up and put an arm around Sarah. "I'll see if I can find Jacob and Amelia. You look done in. While you're resting at Amelia's, I'll see the quartermaster and get our housing assignment."

Emmie turned as a male voice shouted, "Rand!" She hadn't seen Rand's brother Jacob in a while, but she instantly recognized his stocky frame and brown hair.

"Rand!" Jacob ran toward them and seconds later the brothers were hugging and slapping one another on the back. "I can't believe you're here. And Sarah too. Amelia will be ecstatic. She's been driving me crazy with missing Sarah." He pulled her into a bear hug, then his face sobered when he saw Emmie. Rand gave him one last clap on the back and hurried off to find the quartermaster.

Emmie knew Jacob had never liked Ben. She hadn't had much occasion to talk to Jacob herself, so she assumed his reserve was because of her brother. He would just have to find out she wasn't like her brother. She held out her hand. "Hello, Jacob."

He smiled then and took her hand. "Emmie. What are you doing here? Did your husband join the army? Ma wrote when you got married."

Sarah rushed in as Emmie bit her lip. "Emmie's a widow and she's here to keep me company. But there's plenty of time for explanations later. I'm dying to see Amelia. Where is she?"

"I'll show you to our quarters. She's been feeling poorly, and I told her to rest this afternoon."

"What's wrong with her?" Sarah sounded alarmed. She and Emmie hurried to keep up with Jacob's long strides as he led them across the uncompleted parade ground toward a row of wooden houses.

He grinned. "You'll have to ask her."

"You don't mean—"

"Yeah. Can you believe I'm going to be a papa? Rand and I are going to make each other uncles within a few weeks of one another."

Sarah clapped her hands. "Wait until Rand hears!"

"Here we are." He stopped beside a small wooden house.

Emmie looked around curiously. The home was tiny, and sap ran from the cuts and nicks in the logs. She touched a sticky lump and raised it to her nose. It smelled like pine. She'd noticed coming toward the fort that this area had a lot more trees than down around Laramie.

Jacob pushed open the door and led them into a tiny parlor with a fireplace in one wall. It looked much like the home they'd left except it was even smaller. "It doesn't look like much now, I know," he said with an apologetic grin. "I haven't had time to knock together a table and chairs for the kitchen yet, so we've been eating in the parlor. It's pretty inconvenient for Amelia, but I told her I'd make sure I got to it this week. The Indians have been a constant nuisance. Even the wood detail has to be accompanied by armed troops. And that doesn't always stop Red Cloud's band, as I'm sure you noticed on the way in."

"Who was the murdered soldier?" Sarah asked as Jacob led the way through the minuscule kitchen toward the closed door on the far side. "Did I know him?"

"No, Corporal Johnson was a new recruit, and he

was as hotheaded as they come. We're just lucky more weren't killed. Some of the men have been spoiling for a fight, but I thank the good Lord that Carrington has been able to restrain them so far." He pushed open the door to the bedroom and smiled when he saw his wife.

She lay on her side, one arm outflung and her face pink in sleep. Her black hair was unbound and fanned out on the pillow in a silken cloud. Jacob's face softened in love and pride as he gazed at his sleeping wife.

"Honey. Look who's here." He spoke gently as he took her hand.

Her long lashes fluttered and she opened her eyes blearily. She stared for a long minute into Sarah's eyes, then bolted upright. "Sarah?" She looked over at Jacob, then back at Sarah.

Sarah bounded forward and jumped onto the bed. "It's me, Amelia. It's really me."

A pang of jealousy overwhelmed Emmie as she saw Sarah and Amelia fall into each other's arms with tears of joy. She'd always liked Amelia, but she'd grown to rely on Sarah over the past weeks. Bleakly, she knew she would have to settle for second place in Sarah's affections. She squared her shoulders and pushed the hurt feelings away. She would not be like her brother Ben. He had allowed jealousy and possessiveness to ruin his life and Labe's too. She'd come here alone and she could leave the same way if she had to. But she didn't want to leave. It felt grand to laugh with friends like Sarah and Rand.

Amelia drew away and noticed Emmie standing unobtrusively to one side. "Why, dear Emmie too!" She slipped out of the bed and ran to give her a quick hug. "How wonderful to see you. I had no idea you were with Sarah. Is Monroe with you?"

Amelia seemed truly glad to see her. Emmie shook her head at Amelia's question. She glanced gratefully at Sarah, who rushed in with a quick explanation of Emmie's circumstances.

"You poor dear." Amelia gave her another quick hug. "No wonder you look so peaked. I am glad you're here, though you may want to run screaming for home with two crotchety women in delicate conditions for company."

"Well, I'll leave you three to get caught up on all the gossip and go find my brother," Jacob put in.

The women barely noticed his departure as they all three piled on the bed and began to talk at once.

"We brought some fresh newspapers from back East with us—they're only two months old," Sarah said.

"And I brought a magazine of new fashions Margaret sent with me. I've been saving it until winter settled in, but we could get it out whenever you want," Emmie added.

"Let's save it until we can get together with the other ladies," Amelia said. "You'll love our little community. There's Mrs. Horton, the wife of our post surgeon and surgeon in chief of the Mountain District; Mrs. Carrington, the commander's wife; Mrs. Wands; Mrs. Bisbee; and Mrs. Grummond. They've been a wonderful help to me." She slipped off the bed, picked up the hairbrush from the barrel that served as a nightstand, and began to put her hair up. "Let's have some tea and then I'll introduce you to the ladies."

The bugle sounded retreat as Isaac strode through Fort Phil Kearny. It bustled with activity as soldiers led their horses toward the stables and hurried to get ready for evening mess. Isaac thought he'd never seen a more beautiful spot than this Tongue River Valley.

The Bighorn Mountains south of the valley, the Panther Mountains to the west, and the Black Hills to the east all formed a majestic backdrop to this busy little fort in the wilderness.

Black-billed magpies scrabbled in the thin dirt in search of food, while flocks of mountain chickadees chirped in the trees outside the fort. The smell of cut pine and sawdust mingled with the scent of horse and wood smoke as he made his way through the tradesman encampment. The air was fresh with the scent of imminent rain, and Isaac could see thunderheads towering like newly forming mountains to the west.

The stockade was not yet completely finished. Its walls of hewn pine were interspersed with block guardhouses situated diagonally at the corners of the fort, and the gates were made of massive double planks with small sally wickets and a small sally port for the officers' use. Immediately inside was the quartermaster's yard, a cottonwood corral that housed the teamsters and their stock along with wagons, hayricks, and the shops for wagon makers and leather workers. Just beyond that was the fort proper, with officers' row, the barracks, and the sutler's store. He skirted the manure and mud as he hurried toward the Campbell quarters.

Emmie opened the door when he knocked. He grinned at the startled look on her face.

"Isaac. I thought it was Rand." A delicate blush bloomed in her cheeks, and she avoided his eyes.

"He sent me to fetch you two ladies. Your quarters are ready for your inspection." He took out his large white handkerchief and carefully wiped the corner of her mouth. "Jam," he said with a gentle smile. He wished he could kiss it off. She was the cutest little thing.

Emmie had flushed when Isaac showed up at the door. Why did he always have to catch her at such a disadvantage? Besides, she wasn't interested in a flirtation with anyone, no matter how attractive he was. He looked particularly handsome with his auburn hair ruffled by the wind and his face tanned from the sun. Her face flamed as he grinned at her discomfiture.

"I'll get Sarah." She left him standing at the open door as she went to fetch her friend.

"Are our quarters close to Amelia's?" Sarah asked. She and Emmie snatched up their bonnets from the hook near the door and followed Isaac down the steps.

"The permanent ones will be next door."

"Permanent ones? Where are we going now?"

Isaac pointed toward a group of tents in a small open space near the quartermaster's yard.

"You're joking, right?" Sarah stopped and looked up at Isaac in dismay. "Amelia says we'll have snow soon. We can't live in a tent."

"It's just while your quarters are built. We've put a Sibley stove in for you to keep the cold away. Rand tried his best to get you something else. Jacob even offered to let you stay with them, but you saw how small their place is. This is the best the quartermaster could do on short notice."

Sarah bit her lip. "Well, if it's the best he could do, then we have no choice. Please don't say anything to Rand about my being upset."

Isaac glanced at Emmie. "Think you can stand it too?"

"Of course," she said with more certainty than she felt.

He smiled again, and Emmie thought she saw a hint of admiration in his blue eyes, but she pushed the thought away. She didn't want admiration or anything else from him, she told herself firmly.

Rand was busy directing soldiers where to put the barrels of their belongings when they arrived. "I'm sorry, Green Eyes, but this will have to do for now. But it's not too bad. See, we've put three A tents together to make three rooms. We can store our trunks and mess chest in one. You and I can sleep in here, and Emmie can have the next one. Joel is going to stay with the Carringtons until our quarters are ready. There's a stove in Emmie's room too, as well as this one. Will you be all right?"

"Of course. This is very pleasant, Rand." Sarah walked through the interconnected tents with Emmie following close behind. Two army cots and the stove took up most of the space in the Campbells' room, but Emmie would have a bit more floor area for possessions.

"We could use my room as a parlor during the day," Emmie said with a quick look around. She was very conscious of Isaac's nearness as he hovered at her elbow. When he looked at her, she felt as though he was looking into her very soul. Monroe had been all about making her laugh, but Isaac seemed to care about her comfort and happiness.

"You'll probably spend most of your daylight

hours with Amelia and the other ladies," Rand said. "But thanks for the offer."

Sarah and Emmie covered their dismay about their quarters with nervous chatter about the fort and questioned Rand about what he'd learned of the situation.

"I really wish I hadn't brought you both here," he admitted. "Jacob says no one is allowed outside the fort except for fighting and absolute necessities. Troops escort wagon trains occasionally, but Amelia hasn't been outside the stockade in two months. Red Cloud's tactics seem to be constant harassment. There's some kind of skirmish almost every day, and the Indians seem to be getting bolder in their ploys."

"But Amelia said some of the ladies even brought their children with them. It surely can't be that dangerous."

"I think Carrington and headquarters had no idea how strongly the Sioux would object to this fort. They call this harassment the 'Circle of Death.' Jacob says they're determined to drive the whites from here for good."

The bugle sounded mess call and Rand took Sarah's arm. "What's done is done now." He steered her toward the officers' mess hall. "But I want you both to stay away from the stockade walls, and if you're told to get to safety, obey immediately."

Remembering the scalped soldier, Emmie gulped. *Was it as dangerous as it seemed?*

EIGHT

Isaac took Emmie's arm and escorted her to the mess hall. She could feel the smooth muscles of his forearm under his coat sleeve, and she wanted to draw her hand away. To do so would have been rude, though, and it wasn't Isaac's fault that she found him entirely too attractive for her own peace of mind.

By the time they ate the luncheon of ever-present salt pork and beans, reconstituted vegetables, and coffee, the first fat drops of rain had begun to fall. The clouds obscured the sun and cast a dark pall over the fort as the wind howled like a thousand banshees. The men had already left for their afternoon duties, and Emmie glanced at the sky nervously as she and Sarah left the mess hall.

They ran for the safety of Amelia's quarters, with the wind driving sand and cold rain into their skin like a horde of vicious mosquitoes. Soaked and chilled, they burst through the door into Amelia's parlor. As they shook the water out of their clothes and hair, a horrendous pounding and clattering began all around them.

"What's happening?" Emmie cried. She'd never heard anything like it.

They all ran to the front window and looked out on a scene of pandemonium. Horses reared in terror and soldiers fought to control them as man and beast alike were pelted with hail the size of eggs. The white missiles fell so hard they left dents in the soft ground. Several soldiers cringed beneath the blows as their hats went flying. It only lasted for a few minutes, but by the time the freakish weather was over, the post surgeon had several bleeding soldiers to attend to. One man was trampled beneath the hooves of a panicked horse.

The three women worried about the men until Amelia spied her husband under the overhanging roof of the sutler's store. He waved at them cheerily and gave no evidence of dismay, so they assumed everyone was all right.

The next morning Emmie awoke with something tickling her nose. The wind howled through the tent, but she had piled on so many blankets and buffalo robes, she was pleasantly warm and comfortable. She reached up to scratch her nose and touched cold, dry snow. During the night the early snowstorm had arrived, and the wind blew the powdery fluff through the cracks in the tent openings. A thick layer of white covered Emmie and all her possessions.

She sat up and shook the snow from her hair and bedclothes. Scrambling out of bed, she emptied the snow from her shoes. She felt oddly lightheaded as she shook her dress thoroughly and pulled her nightgown over her head. By the time she was dressed, she was shivering almost uncontrollably. As she bent over to tie her boots, she almost tumbled to the floor as a wave of dizziness washed over her. She straightened up, suddenly overwhelmed with an attack of nausea.

She rushed to the chamber pot at the end of her cot and vomited into it.

What on earth was wrong with her? She couldn't get sick now, not with Sarah and Amelia to care for. Clutching the chamber pot weakly, she sank back on the bunk. Amelia and Sarah both felt poorly so often. Who would clean up and cook if she fell ill?

As she thought of their condition, a terrible thought made her gasp. When did she have her last monthly? Another wave of nausea shook her as she slumped against the pillow and thought about it. She hadn't had her monthly at all in August, and September's should have arrived last week. She closed her eyes as she contemplated the possibility that she might be pregnant. It could be, couldn't it? Tears trickled from beneath her closed eyes. Was there no end to her shame? Did she now have to bear a bastard child? Surely not. This was probably just a result of being chilled in the night— or perhaps the influenza, or maybe even cholera. Anything, even something deadly, would be preferable to what she suspected was true.

Sarah had evidently heard her retching, for she scratched at the opening between the two tents. "Emmie? Are you all right? I'm coming in." She didn't wait for an answer but pushed open the flap and entered. She hurried straight to the bed where Emmie lay, bleakly contemplating how much to tell her friend.

"I'm fine. Just a little sick feeling. It's probably nothing."

Sarah stared hard at Emmie and frowned. "You're much too pale, Emmie. Rand, please ask Dr. Horton to stop by," she called to her husband, who hovered near the doorway. "I don't like the way she looks. And get the fire going in the stove too, please." She turned back to Emmie. "Now I want you to get back in your night-gown and into bed. It's my turn to take care of you."

"I'm feeling much better. Maybe if I had a cracker and some tea—" Emmie stammered.

"The very thing. That always helps me when I feel sick. I'll be right back with some, and I want to find you snuggled in the covers when I return." With a last admonishing wag of her finger, Sarah stepped through the tent flap.

Wearily Emmie pulled off her clothes and tugged on her thick flannel nightgown. There was no use in protesting. Little Sarah could be implacable when she thought she was in the right.

Sarah returned with the steaming tea and a tin

of crackers at the same time Dr. Horton arrived with his black bag. He was a tall, spare man in his forties, with a balding pate and a pleasant smile and demeanor. "Well, now, what seems to be the matter, young lady? You should be up and about. That pretty face of yours is good for morale." He set his bag down on the bed and drew out his stethoscope. Rand came in just behind him and began to poke at the coals in the stove.

Sarah handed the tea and crackers to Emmie. "I'll run over and get Amelia while the doctor's with you."

"There's really no need—" But Sarah was gone before Emmie could finish her protest. Rand followed her out after winking at Emmie kindly.

"When did you start feeling poorly?" The doctor put the cold stethoscope against her chest.

"Just this morning." She bent forward obediently as he placed the stethoscope on her back and listened intently. She answered the rest of his questions and lay back against the pillow as he probed around on her stomach.

"Ah," he said after a few moments.

"What is it?"

"When did you have your last monthly?"

Oh no. She swallowed hard, then told him in a hoarse whisper.

He nodded. "I'd say you're increasing. The little one should arrive about mid-May." He frowned when he noticed her obvious distress. "You don't seem overjoyed."

"My husband is dead, Dr. Horton, and I have no family."

He nodded again. "Yes, I know. But at least you're among friends. And I'm sure in a fort full of eligible men, you could find a father for your baby if you wished."

"I'm not interested in marrying again," she whispered. The doctor raised his eyebrows at her answer, and she laid a hand on his arm. "You've been very kind. How long will the sickness last?"

"Hard to say." He stood and began to put his things back in his bag. "It could only be for a few weeks or a few months. If you're really unlucky, it could last your entire pregnancy. But most women find it subsides after four or five weeks." He gestured at the crackers in her hand. "Those usually help if you keep some beside your bed and nibble on them before you even get out of bed. I would suggest you stay in bed today—you've had quite a shock, and I can see it's upset you. If you need me again, just send one of the men for me." He patted her hand. "At least you won't be alone any longer. God knows best, my dear." With a final pat he hurried away.

Emmie closed her eyes and a few tears slipped out from under her lashes. It was easy for him to say that God knew best. The doctor wasn't alone in the world. She had no means of supporting herself, let alone a baby. What was she going to do? Rand and Sarah wouldn't throw her out, but she was supposed to be here to help Sarah, not be an additional burden on her friends who'd been so kind. She had no skills, no resources. She shuddered from the hopelessness of her situation.

Why did she ever have to meet Monroe?

She turned her head as Sarah and Amelia hurried into her tent. Amelia looked as anxious as Sarah did, and Emmie felt a wave of love for both friends. They truly did care about her. She didn't know why they should, but they did, and she was grateful to both of them.

"What did the doctor say?" Sarah laid a cool hand on Emmie's forehead.

Emmie bit her lip. There was no use trying to keep it from them. "I'm going to have a baby."

Sarah's eyes widened and she gaped before she recovered her composure. "Oh, that's wonderful! You'll never be alone again. When?"

"May."

Never alone. She hadn't thought of what a difference a baby would make.

Sarah handed her a crust of bread. "A baby would have made Monroe adore you even more. I'm sorry he's not going to meet his child. But you'll be a wonderful mother, Emmie. The best. And your baby will love you even more than Monroe did."

Amelia clapped her hands in delight. "It will be such fun for us to raise our babies together. We'll have all kinds of good advice for you by the time the wee one arrives."

Emmie was grateful for the way they were hiding the dismay they both must have felt. "I'll be fine in a day or two, and I promise not to be a bother, Sarah. I'm supposed to be helping you."

"Oh, pishposh, I don't need any help. I just needed company. You'll be even better company now that you know what we're going through."

"But what will Rand say?"

"What do you mean?" Sarah seemed genuinely puzzled. "What could he say? He loves kids." She fluffed up Emmie's pillow and pushed her down against it. "Now you just quit your fretting and get some rest. Everything is going to be just fine. You'll see."

Emmie allowed herself to be tucked into the quilts and furs as the fire in the stove threw out welcome warmth and cheeriness. She didn't know what the future might hold, but with friends like the Campbells, it would surely be all right.

But this would end any interest Isaac might have in her.

A VACATION TO SUNSET COVE WAS HER WAY OF
celebrating and thanking her parents. After all,
Claire Dellamore's childhood was like a fairytale.
But with the help of Luke Elwell, Claire discovers
that fairytale was really an elaborate lie . . .

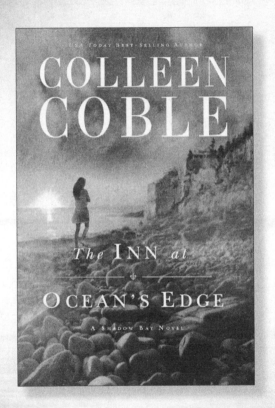

THE FIRST SUNSET COVE NOVEL

COLLEEN LOVES TO HEAR FROM HER READERS!

Be sure to sign up for Colleen's newsletter for insider information on deals and appearances.

Visit her website at www.colleencoble.com
Twitter: @colleencoble
Facebook: colleencoblebooks

THOMAS NELSON
Since 1798

About the Author

Photo by Clik Chick Photography

R ITA finalist Colleen Coble is the author of several bestselling romantic suspense novels, including *Tidewater Inn*, and the Mercy Falls, Lonestar, and Rock Harbor series.